Daniel Visits a Pumpkin Patch

By Maggie Testa

Poses and layouts by Jason Fruchter

Ready-to-Read

Simon Spotlight

New York   London   Toronto   Sydney   New Delhi

SIMON SPOTLIGHT
An imprint of Simon & Schuster Children's Publishing Division
1230 Avenue of the Americas, New York, New York 10020
This Simon Spotlight edition July 2021
© 2021 The Fred Rogers Company.
For information about special discounts for bulk purchases, please contact Simon & Schuster Special
Sales at 1-866-506-1949 or business@simonandschuster.com.
Manufactured in the United States of America 0521 LAK
2 4 6 8 10 9 7 5 3 1
ISBN 978-1-5344-8664-5 (hc)
ISBN 978-1-5344-8663-8 (pbk)
ISBN 978-1-5344-8665-2 (eBook)

Hi, neighbor!

I am at a pumpkin patch.

Have you ever gone to a pumpkin patch?

"Find the one you like best," says Mom.

Which pumpkin
would you pick?

Here is Miss Elaina.

"Hi, Daniel," she says.

"Look at my pumpkin. It is the perfect pumpkin for me."

"I like your pumpkin,"
I tell her.
"Which one should I pick?"

"That pumpkin is nice, but it is too big for me," I say.

Here is Prince Wednesday.

"Hi, Daniel and

Miss Elaina," he says.

"Look at my pumpkin. It is the perfect pumpkin for me."

I take another look
around the pumpkin patch.

"There it is," I say. "There is the perfect pumpkin for me."

"I like your pumpkin," says Miss Elaina.

"Me too!"

says Prince Wednesday.

At home I put my pumpkin in front of our house.

It is the perfect pumpkin
for our family.